THE CRY OF
THE OCELOT

THE UNOFFICIAL ANIMAL WARRIORS
OF THE OVERWORLD SERIES

THE CRY OF
THE OCELOT

AN UNOFFICIAL MINECRAFTERS NOVEL
BOOK TWO

Maya Grace

Sky Pony Press
New York

THE UNOFFICIAL ANIMAL WARRIORS OF THE OVERWORLD
SERIES: THE CRY OF THE OCELOT.

Copyright © 2019 by Hollan Publishing, Inc.

Minecraft® is a registered trademark of Notch Development AB.
The Minecraft game is copyright © Mojang AB.

Sky Pony Press books may be purchased in bulk at special discounts for sales
promotion, corporate gifts, fund-raising, or educational purposes. Special
editions can also be created to specifications. For details, contact the Special
Sales Department, Sky Pony Press, 307 West 36th Street, 11th Floor,
New York, NY 10018 or info@skyhorsepublishing.com.

Sky Pony® is a registered trademark of Skyhorse Publishing, Inc.®,
a Delaware corporation.

Visit our website at www.skyponypress.com.

10 9 8 7 6 5 4 3 2 1

Library of Congress Cataloging-in-Publication Data is available on file.

Special thanks to Erin L. Falligant.

Cover illustration by Amanda Brack
Cover design by Brian Peterson

Hardcover ISBN: 978-1-5107-4134-8
E-book ISBN: 978-1-5107-4139-3

Printed in the United States of America

TABLE OF CONTENTS

CHAPTER 1

link, clink, clink!

Ella slid her helmet from the anvil and held it out in front of her. Sure enough, the helmet cast off a faint purple glow. "Enchanted with Respiration," she whispered.

At her feet, her wolf-dog, Taiga, whined.

"I know, buddy," said Ella, reaching down to stroke his silver-gray fur. "Breathing underwater scares me too. But we might need this someday. Someday *soon.*"

Days were growing shorter. Nights were growing longer. More hostile mobs were spawning across the Overworld. And Gran had told Ella and her cousins that they needed to be ready—ready to fight.

Ella shivered, remembering the zombie pigmen she had fought to save her wolf only a few weeks ago. She had named him Taiga because that was where she'd found him, all alone in the cold biome.

That was where he led me, she remembered, by howling to her across the plains. He had chosen her. He had called to her. And she had listened.

Just like my mom, thought Ella, a smile playing at the corners of her mouth. She'd barely known her mother. She'd been killed in the Uprising, when the day and night cycle stopped and hostile mobs spawned uncontrollably across the Overworld. But Gran said Ella's mother had been a "wolf-whisperer," too.

Ella squatted beside Taiga, gazing into his golden eyes. "I'll never let anything happen to you," she said, kissing his snout. "I'll protect you. I promise."

He whined and gave her chin a lick, as if to say, *I'll protect you too.* And she knew he would.

As Ella stood, she tucked her hair behind her ear and reached for another weapon. She and her cousin Rowan had lugged a box of swords, bows, and armor all the way from Gran's mansion down to the garden shed, where Ella could enchant them with an anvil. But as she poked through the pieces, she wondered, *Can I really use these? Will I have the courage?*

She blew a cobweb off an old bow before placing it in the anvil. Then she reached into her box of enchanted books. "Flame, Infinity, Power, Punch," she murmured as she sorted the books. " She finally settled on "Infinity." But before she could slide the book into the anvil, something shot through the window and whizzed by her head.

She hit the floor of the shed, her heart pounding. Beside her, Taiga growled and sprang to his feet.

Ella held her breath, trying not to make a sound. *What was that? A skeleton arrow?* She crawled ever so slowly to a crack in the wall of the shed. As she peered through the crack, she saw *boots*. Jogging toward the shed. Fast.

Ella recognized those boots.

"Rowan!"

She jumped up just as her older cousin burst through the door, her red ponytail swinging side to side.

"Sorry!" called Rowan. "So sorry! Did I hit you?"

Ella ran a hand over her head, as if checking for a bump or wound. "No! But you sure came close. Was that an arrow?"

"No, a trident," Rowan said. "Gran and I were just testing it out." She crossed the shed and reached for something stuck in the wall. It looked like a spear with three prongs—three very *sharp* prongs.

"Yikes," said Ella under her breath. "You need to work on your aim. You could do some damage with that!"

"I know," said Rowan. "Especially if you enchant it with something. Will you?"

Ella sighed. "I'm kind of busy here," she said. But as she gestured toward the boxes of books and weapons behind her, a shadow fell across the floor.

"What time is it?" she asked Rowan, checking the sky through the window.

Rowan's face darkened. "Early," she said. "Too early. It's not even five o'clock, and the sun is starting to sink."

The two cousins locked eyes. *Gran was right,* thought Ella. The day-night cycle was shifting, ever so slowly—a sign of another Uprising to come.

She swallowed hard. "Give me that," she said, gesturing toward the trident. "I'll find an enchantment for it."

Rowan nodded and handed over the trident, which was much heavier than Ella had expected. No wonder Rowan was having trouble throwing it! And those prongs were *so* sharp. Ella set it down carefully on top of her pile of weapons.

The she fingered through her enchanted books. "Hmm . . ." she thought out loud. "Which enchantments work with tridents?"

"I don't know," said Rowan as she squatted to give Taiga a head scratch. "That's your department."

Ella's chest puffed with pride, just a little. She *had* become a master of enchantments. Even Gran said so. But Ella had never enchanted a trident. "We'll have to ask Gran," she said with a sigh.

While Rowan went to fetch Gran, Ella stepped to the door to watch her go. Shadows fell across the courtyard. They spilled over Gran's garden, filled with spindly sugar cane and wheat, and melons and pumpkins on winding vines. The shadows crept up the obsidian wall that protected the mansion from the world outside. And as Ella watched, the shadows reached out toward the fishing pond, as if nudging her cousin Jack on the shoulder to say, "Time to put that fishing pole away."

Fishing was all Jack ever did anymore. With his

enchanted fishing pole and a pond that Gran kept stocked with fish, he caught fish after fish after fish. *He's going to drain the pond!* thought Ella, blowing out a breath of frustration.

Couldn't her younger cousin see that there were more important things to do around here? Things to *prepare* for?

As she strode out of the shed to tell him so, Taiga leaped up to follow.

"Jack!" Ella had to call twice before his head finally spun around.

"What?" As he pulled the red hood of his sweatshirt off his head, a tuft of dark hair sprang up.

"Why don't you do something useful?" she asked. "You should be learning how to use a bow—or a trident, like Rowan."

He shook his head. "I'm fishing." As if to make his point, his line suddenly went taut. He yanked it back, and a yellow pufferfish leaped out of the water.

Ella was surprised to see Jack unhook the fish from his line and cast it back into the water.

"I thought you used pufferfish for your potions," she said.

He shrugged. "I'm hoping for a salmon."

Ella scoffed. "There aren't any in there! Gran stocked the pond with pufferfish," she said.

Jack set his jaw. "There are some salmon in here too," he said. "Gran said so."

Ella's toe started tapping—she couldn't help it. "We don't need salmon," she said. "Gran's already making dinner. Why don't you help me by feeding Taiga or something?"

Taiga barked his approval and nudged Jack's arm. But Jack didn't even glance up. "I told you—I'm fishing."

Poor Taiga whined and sat on his rump. He'd been trying to win Jack over for the last couple of weeks, but Jack would barely say hello to the dog.

Why? Ella wondered, as she had so many times since she'd tamed her wolf-dog. *Is he jealous?*

Jack couldn't communicate with wolves, the way Ella could. And he couldn't communicate with horses, the way Rowan and Gran could. When Gran had told the cousins about the special gifts they'd inherited from their parents and from her, Jack had felt left out—Ella could tell.

But he was a genius at brewing potions, like his mother had been! She was a scientist who had traveled all over the Overworld, collecting potion ingredients. And Gran had given Jack his mother's old journals, filled with potion brewing "recipes" inside.

Jack should be down in the basement right now, brewing up a storm. So why did he seem so down?

Maybe because he thinks he'll never have his own animal friend, Ella thought sadly as she pulled Taiga into her arms.

The back door of the mansion suddenly opened with a *bang,* and Rowan came flying down the steps. "Gran's coming!" she called.

Ella stood up and tried one more time. "Jack," she

said, "come help me enchant the trident, will you? Gran and I will teach you how."

This time, he didn't even respond.

"Fine," she snapped, turning on her heel. "Suit yourself."

But as the beacon overhead flickered on, lighting up the courtyard, Ella thought of the hostile mobs that were probably spawning outside those obsidian walls right now.

And she worried about Jack, as she always did. Gran had *taught* her to look out for him.

If Jack doesn't learn how to use weapons, Ella thought, *how will he survive the Uprising? How will Rowan and I protect him?*

She fought the wave of panic rising in her chest, and hurried toward the garden shed.

CHAPTER 2

Gran adjusted the glasses on her nose and slid her finger down the tiny print in her enchantment book.

"Loyalty or Riptide," she said as she snapped the book shut. "Those are the only two enchantments that will work with a trident."

Ella's shoulders slumped. "I don't have those," she said. "I have everything else, but I don't have those."

"Are you sure?" Gran turned toward the box of enchanted books on the floor of the shed.

"I'm sure," said Ella. She knew the books in that box like the back of her hand—the way Gran knew every square inch of her garden.

Gran sighed. "Well, then, I guess we're going to have to get lots of practice with the trident. If you're skilled enough at fighting with it, we won't need an enchantment."

As Gran reached for the weapon, Ella marveled again at how much her grandmother had changed over the last few weeks. She had once spent her days cooking in the kitchen, singing to her jukebox. Now she was teaching them to fight with dangerous weapons. Her long silver hair, which had once flowed down over her cyan-colored robes, was bound in a tight braid. And those robes? They'd been replaced by sturdy pants and boots.

With the trident in her hands, Gran looked ready to fight. Like a warrior. *Like Rowan,* Ella suddenly realized.

But Gran didn't hand the trident to Rowan.

"It's Ella's turn," she said with an encouraging smile, suddenly looking like the old Gran again.

Ella took the weapon, holding it awkwardly in her hands. "Do I use it like a sword?" she asked.

Gran nodded. "You can," she said. "Or throw it like a spear."

Ella caught Rowan's eye and grimaced, remembering how Rowan's "spear" had come right through the garden shed window. She shook her head. "I'm better with a sword," she said.

She stepped out of the garden shed into the courtyard, where she had more room. As she gently swung the trident from side to side, she flashed back on the zombie pigmen that she had fought off with her sword in the Taiga. Just the thought made her heart thud in her ears.

But I had an enchanted sword then, she remembered.

Enchanted with Flame. And still, she'd barely survived—barely managed to save her wolf, and herself. *So how will I fight with a heavy trident,* she wondered. *A trident with no enchantments at all?*

When Rowan finally reached for the trident, Ella gladly handed it over. "I think I'll stick with my sword," she said.

But a wave of worry crossed Gran's face. "Ella, you'll need to know how to use *lots* of weapons," she said sternly. "Don't quit so soon."

Ella turned away, feeling shame creep up her cheeks. When she saw Jack, still fishing, she pointed. "What about him?" she asked. "Doesn't he need to practice too?"

Gran reached for Ella's hand. "Shh," she said. "Leave Jack be for now. We'll prepare him, too, in time."

But as the clock tower *bonged* overhead, Ella jumped. It was only six o'clock, and already, a blanket of darkness had fallen over the Overworld.

In time? Ella wanted to say. *We're running out of time!*

Like thunderclouds approaching the plains, the Uprising was coming—Ella could *feel* it. And there was no stopping it now.

* * *

Before crawling into bed, Ella pulled her long, brunette hair into a ponytail. Then she settled back against her pillow and patted the side of her mattress.

Instantly, Taiga sprang onto the bed. He spun in a tight circle before settling in, nestled against Ella's side.

"Good boy," she said, resting her hand on his head.

Only a month ago, she'd laid in this very bed, listening to Taiga howling to her from so far away. Howling for *help*.

But now the Overworld fell silent. She held her breath, listening for *anything*—the whine of another wolf. The hiss of a creeper. The moan of a zombie.

They were out there right now, she knew. *But I'm safe inside the walls of Gran's mansion,* Ella reminded herself. *At least for now.*

She tried to sleep, shaking off her worries from the day the way Taiga shook off water after a swim in the fishpond. And slowly, she felt herself drift to her peaceful place. She floated above the earth, as if she'd just drank one of Jack's potions of Leaping.

Then something jolted her awake.

Ella sat up straight, her body shaking.

She listened, waiting. And then she heard it again!

A low growl came from the corner of her room. Then a scratching against the wooden door.

Taiga!

He'd heard something, and he was ready to fight.

* * *

"Taiga, shh!" Ella cried, sliding out of bed and racing across the floor.

As she knelt beside him, she felt the ridge of fur

spring up along his back. Taiga was frightened, or maybe angry. But why?

She listened for him to tell her. She squeezed her eyes shut. But he only pawed at the door as if to say, "Let's go. Now!"

So she opened the door.

Taiga flew down the hall toward Jack's room. Ella followed, wondering if she should grab a weapon or a book or anything hard she could use to defend herself.

Then she realized Taiga was leading her into Jack's room. Was Jack okay?

Ella raced through the doorway just behind Taiga, quickly flipping on the redstone switch.

The torch lit up the room, which was empty. Jack's bed was perfectly made, as if he'd not been in it. As if he hadn't gone to bed at all.

"Jack!" Ella called softly. She checked his closet, and then the hall behind her. Where was he?

"Show me, Taiga," she said. "Show me where Jack went!"

The wolf-dog whined and trotted down the hall. Around one corner, and then another. Down the set of stairs toward the kitchen. And toward the basement door.

There, Ella hesitated. Jack's brewing stand was in the basement, and that's probably exactly where he was right now. *At least he'd better be,* she thought, crossing her fingers. But the basement was the *last* place Ella wanted to go in the middle of the night.

She pictured the cobwebs, the mossy steps, the

silverfish that lived in the cracks and crevices of the stone stairwell.

But Taiga whined at the door, urging her on.

"Aw, Jack," Ella sighed, pushing open the door. "You'd better have a good reason for being down there."

She was glad to see the torch burning brightly, lighting her way. But as she took her first step down, the stone beneath her foot felt ice-cold. And a draft sent a wave of goosebumps across her skin.

She pushed through a cobweb and hurried downward, ready to get this hunt for Jack over with and get back to bed.

"He probably lost track of time," she told herself, speaking out loud so that she wouldn't feel so alone. Her voice echoed off the cobblestone walls of the circular staircase.

When she reached the bottom, Taiga had already pushed his way through the door into the brewing room.

Ella fumbled to find the redstone switch, hoping to see Jack's head bowed over his brewing stand.

But once again, the room was empty.

Taiga padded around, sniffing at the ground. Ella hurried after him. "Jack?" she called. And then louder. "Jack, where are you?"

No one answered.

Then Ella's gaze shifted to the shelves in the corner, where Jack liked to proudly display his potions.

The shelf was nearly empty. The potions were gone.

And now Ella knew for certain.

Jack was gone too.

CHAPTER 3

Ella paused to catch her breath at the top of the basement stairs. She glanced wildly from side to side, wondering which way to turn. Left, to go to Gran's room? Or right, to race up another three sets of stairs to Rowan's bedroom in the high turret?

She turned right.

But as she wound her way up the stairs, her legs felt *so* heavy, as if she were trying to run in a dream—or nightmare. As if she had run through a patch of soul sand in the Nether, or been hit by one of Jack's splash potions of slowness.

Finally, she reached the top. "Rowan!" she called, before she'd even reached the bedroom door.

Taiga squeezed through the door to get ahead of her, as usual. When the wolf-dog jumped onto Rowan's bed, Rowan groaned.

"Taiga, *no,*" she whined, pulling her pillow over her face.

Ella pulled it right back off. "Rowan, wake up. Wake up!"

"What?" She pushed a mass of red hair off her face and squinted into the moonlight.

"Jack's gone."

That did it. Rowan snapped to attention. "What do you mean *gone?*"

"He didn't go to bed last night. He's not in the basement. And *all* of his potions are gone off the shelf."

Rowan jumped up and ran to the window, as if she might find him sitting beside the pond, calmly fishing.

"Where would he go?" she asked.

Ella shrugged. The only time Jack had left the mansion was when she and Rowan had set off for the Taiga to find her wolf. He had followed them, using his potion of invisibility.

But where would he go on his own—in the middle of the night? And *why?*

"Should we wake Gran?" she asked, biting her lip.

Rowan hesitated. She glanced out the window again, and then turned back. "Yes," she said. "We should definitely wake Gran. She'll know what to do."

*   *   *

Gran made them search the entire house for Jack. But it wasn't until they met back in the kitchen, where the jukebox played an eerie tune, that they found the note.

Ella saw it first: a rolled-up piece of paper stuck inside an empty potion bottle.

As she slid it out, she immediately recognized Jack's messy handwriting—and felt a pang in her heart. She read the note out loud, trying to hold her voice steady:

Dear Gran,
I've gone to the jungle. My mother said I should—she wrote it in her journal. An ocelot might be hurt, and I have to find the temple. My mom said I had to go before it was too late.
Don't worry about me. I have my potions.

Jack

"Ocelot?" said Rowan.

"Temple?" asked Ella, hearing her voice rise.

Gran's face drained of color. "I should never have given him the journals!" she cried. "I didn't know his mother had left him a message inside."

Ella fought back guilty thoughts of her own. *I accused him of fishing too much—of not helping us,* she remembered. But all the while, he had been planning his own journey.

How did I not know? she wondered, fighting tears. *How did I miss the clues?*

Rowan abruptly turned off the jukebox, bringing Ella and Gran to attention. "So let's go after him," she said in her take-charge kind of way. "We need to bring him home, right?"

"Yes." Gran's eyes flashed, and she sprang into action. "Rowan, gather our weapons. Ella, search for any potions Jack might have left in the basement—we'll need them. I'll pack some food."

They divided, each running in a different direction. Taiga followed Ella back downstairs. But what would be left in Jack's brewing room? Anything?

She quickly scanned the shelves, searching for a potion of healing, harming, swiftness, slowness—any one of them would do. She and Rowan had learned during their trip to the Taiga that Jack's potions could *really* come in handy.

But there was nothing left. Not a single bottle.

Jack's backpack was gone from its hook, and his fishing rod too. His tackle box was open, with only a few lures left scattered inside. And Ella noticed the dusty outline of a pickaxe on the wall. Jack had brought a weapon—but it was such a tiny one!

She turned back to the brewing stand, where one of Jack's potion-brewing books lay open. She stepped closer, squinting to make out the text at the top of the page.

Potion of water breathing.

Ella's stomach sunk. Water breathing? But Jack didn't even know how to swim!

The Jack that Ella knew might run into the water without thinking. He would pretend to be brave, even if he wasn't. He would use up his potions *way* too quickly.

Ella slammed the book shut and tore back up the

stairs. If Jack was heading toward the jungle, they had to find him—*fast*. Before he got in over his head . . .

* * *

Ella stood just outside the front door, waiting.

The last time she had left the house in the middle of the night, it had been to follow the howling of her wolf. She and Rowan had run north: across the plains, through a dense forest, all the way to the extreme hills and to the cold Taiga beyond.

But tonight? They'd be going south. Through the swamp. Toward the jungle. To a part of the Overworld she had never seen before.

And Ella was scared.

If she inched her way left on the front porch, she could catch some of the light from the beacon that lit up the courtyard. That yellow light felt safe and warm. Nothing bad could spawn in the light.

But in her heavy armor, stepping left felt difficult. When her backpack scraped against the stone, the iron golem just outside the front gate spun his head. His eyes were dark and watchful beneath his heavy brow.

"It's only me, Golem," said Ella. "It's okay."

But nothing was really okay. Because it wasn't the middle of the night. It was nearly morning, and yet the sun showed no signs of coming up.

Rowan pushed her way out the door behind Ella, loaded down with her own heavy armor and weapons. Taiga followed, as if to say, *Don't leave me behind!* He wagged his silver tail and ran to lick Ella's hand—the only part of her not covered in armor.

When Gran stepped outside, Ella did a double-take. She'd never seen Gran in armor before, and yet her grandmother seemed to move easily in her helmet, chestplate, and leggings.

Gran has fought before, Ella remembered. *She knows what she's doing.*

That thought gave Ella some comfort. That, and having Taiga by her side. Because her *wolf* was a warrior too.

Gran lit her torch. Then she waved the girls toward the front gate.

Time to go, thought Ella. Time to leave the light-filled grounds and safety of the mansion behind. Time to head into the darkness.

She swallowed hard. "C'mon, Taiga. Let's go."

CHAPTER 4

Taiga didn't follow. He preferred to lead the way. He'd run ahead a few feet, sniffing Jack's trail, and then turn around and bark, begging Ella to follow.

"Try to keep him quiet," said Gran. "We don't want him calling attention to us. There are mobs all around, even if we can't see or hear them yet."

Ella called Taiga to her side and then squinted, trying to see across the dark hillside. As she listened for the *hiss* of a creeper or the *moan* of a zombie, fear pricked at the back of her neck.

Lights shone from the village at the base of the hill, beckoning them onward. Ella could almost make out the well, and the gravel roads extending like spokes from a wheel toward the corners of the village.

But Taiga wasn't leading them toward town.

"Shouldn't we stop for supplies?" asked Rowan, pointing toward the village.

"No." Gran's response was so sharp, Ella jumped. Beside her, Taiga whined.

"Why not?" asked Rowan. She stopped walking.

When Gran didn't answer, Rowan spoke louder. "Is it because some of the villagers think you're a witch?"

Ella froze. It was the kind of clumsy question Jack would have asked, except Jack wasn't here to ask it. What was Rowan thinking?

"No," said Gran, her voice strained. "We're not stopping, because we have everything we need. We have food. We have weapons. We have each other. And we have to hurry if we're going to catch up with Jack. So keep moving please, Rowan."

Gran had shut down the conversation, just like that. But Ella knew that what Rowan had said was true—Gran had told the girls herself not long ago. Some of the villagers *did* think Gran was a witch, because she could talk to animals.

Just like me, Ella realized. *I talk to my wolf. If the villagers find out, will they think I'm a witch too?*

When Taiga veered right, giving the village a wide berth, Ella followed.

* * *

As the ground softened beneath Ella's feet, she hurried to catch up with the others. "Is this the swamp?" she whispered to Gran.

"It is," said Gran. "And Taiga is telling us that Jack passed through here."

Taiga was sniffing the ground furiously, darting left and right along the perimeter of the water. *Oh, no,* thought Ella as she studied the swamp. *Please tell me Jack didn't try out his potion of water breathing here!*

She stepped forward, scanning the murky gray water. Lily pads dotted the surface, and a patch of sugar cane sprouted along one end. But there was no sign of Jack.

As a gentle rain began to fall, Ella's breathing slowed. She looked skyward. Would the sun come up soon? No. A full moon shone bright from behind the drifting clouds.

"Will the moon keep mobs from spawning?" she asked Gran.

Gran shook her head. "Slimes spawn in moonlight," she said. "Listen for the sound—you'll know it when you hear it."

Ella froze, listening. She tightened her grip on her sword.

Then Rowan stopped walking so quickly, Ella bumped right into her. "What?" she asked, craning her neck to see around her cousin.

Rowan pointed toward the swamp. "Witch hut," she whispered.

Ella could barely see the outline of the hut. It was built on stilts, like a tree house, and very small—a single room maybe. The window of the hut was dark as night. But Ella couldn't help wondering . . . was a witch inside, staring out? Was she waiting for them to get closer so she could attack them with a deadly splash potion?

Two orange eyes peered at Ella from the deck of the hut. They blinked slowly. Ella caught the swish of a cat tail, and then it was gone.

That's when she heard it. *Squish, slop, squish, slop, squish, slop* . . . Where was it coming from?

"Slime!" cried Rowan. "There!" She whirled around and pointed toward the tree line, just as a giant slime burst out, hopping across the swamp.

Squish, slop, squish, slop, squish . . . smack!

Before Ella could even draw her sword, Gran's arrow hit the slime dead center.

But instead of falling, the slime broke into pieces. Smaller slimes bounced forward now. Three, maybe four of them.

As Ella raised her sword, preparing for battle, Taiga raced ahead of her, growling. He snapped at a slime, squishing it in his jaws until green goo oozed down his muzzle.

Rowan sprinted forward too. She hit a slime with her trident—twice, before Ella was close enough to make her first strike.

I'm too slow! she realized. But she did carry an enchanted sword. As she swung the sword, the slime burst into flames. Hot, steamy slime ran in rivers across the ground.

As Ella spun in a circle, more mini slimes attacked from all directions. Green globs stuck to her leggings and her boots. She flicked them off with her fingers, while Taiga nipped at them with his teeth.

When the last slime was finally gone, Ella sank to her knees. "Rowan? Gran?" she called into the darkness.

"Here!" Rowan was circling the site of the battle, her bow still drawn. She kicked at a slimeball, dropped by the mob she'd just killed.

Slimeballs littered the ground—two here, three there. "Should we collect them?" asked Ella. "To make magma cream for Jack's potions?"

Rowan shook her head. "We don't have a crafting table," she said. "Or a brewing stand. They'll just weigh us down."

Ella sighed. *What a waste.* Jack would have been thrilled to see so many potion ingredients in one place. She picked up one slimeball—just one—and slid it into her backpack for Jack.

Then she saw Gran squatting at the edge of the water.

"Are you hurt?" Ella cried, racing to her grandmother's side.

"No, dear," said Gran. "I've just made a discovery."

There, by the water's edge, was a pile of broken glass. Ella could see the neck of a bottle, cracked in half, and a cork lying on its side a few feet away.

"I think your cousin had a battle of his own," Gran said, lifting the cork tenderly from the ground. She spun it in her fingertips to show Ella. The cork was inscribed with the letter "J."

Oh, no. Jack!

"Did he fight a slime?" asked Ella, her voice tight. But even as she said the words, she knew it hadn't been a slime. The ground here was clear and dry. There were no slime balls. No green smears of slime. No traces at all.

Gran didn't answer, but Ella could practically read her mind.

Jack didn't fight a slime. Jack fought a witch.

She sucked in her breath and glanced back at the witch hut. It was still dark. But something flitted across the window.

Her eyes darted back to the glass on the ground. "Do you think Jack won?" she whispered.

Gran sighed. "I don't know. Witches are very difficult to beat."

So is Jack! Ella wanted to say. She'd seen him with his splash potions in the Taiga. She wanted to believe, desperately, that he was okay. So she searched the ground for proof. For Jack's footsteps, walking away. For a spider eye or sprinkle of gunpowder—something a defeated witch might drop. For *anything*.

That's when Ella heard the unmistakable sound of breaking glass.

CHAPTER 5

The witch stood on the deck of her hut, her arm coiled backward. She was already launching another splash potion from within the folds of her dark robe.

Ella ducked as the bottle smacked against the ground and shattered, potion bubbles rising into the air.

"Take cover!" cried Gran, pulling Ella up by her shirt sleeve. As they raced toward the trees, Ella's boots sank into the wet earth, threatening to pull her down.

When she glanced over her shoulder, she saw Rowan, poised on the beach with her bow drawn. And her first arrow found its mark.

The witch toppled backward. But even as she fell, she was guzzling a potion of healing. And then she was on her feet again—ready to throw another splash potion.

Ella watched in horror as the bottle soared, top over bottom, across the swamp. It struck Rowan's shoulder and broke, just as she dove for the ground.

"Rowan!"

By the time Ella reached her cousin, Rowan was struggling to sit. "Watch . . . out," she said, raising her arm ever so slowly toward the witch hut.

But when Ella turned to look, the witch was already disappearing into the hut. She cackled, her laughter echoing in the night air, and then the door slammed shut.

Rowan tried to stand, but it was as if she were encased in soul sand. "Potion . . . of . . . slow . . . ness," she said wearily.

Then Gran was beside them. "Help me get her into the woods," she said. She took Rowan by one arm, and Ella took the other. Together, they staggered toward the trees.

When they were tucked safely behind a tree, its bark dotted with mushrooms, Gran rummaged through her backpack. "I wish we had potions!" she said. "We desperately need Jack's potion of healing."

Rowan tried to shake her head, but she could only turn it side to side. "I'm . . . oh . . . kay," she said.

Only she wasn't.

Gran made Rowan drink a bottle of milk, slowly so that she wouldn't choke. And finally, the color began returning to her cheeks.

"We need to go," she said, pushing herself to her feet. "We're running out of time!"

"Let Taiga pick up Jack's scent again," Gran instructed Ella.

So Ella walked with her wolf-dog, backtracking along the water's edge. All the while, she kept her eyes trained on the witch hut. And Taiga kept his nose to the ground.

When his tail wagged, she could tell that he'd found Jack's trail. He followed it forward, past a few slimeballs and past broken glass. But then . . . the trail ran out.

It stopped cold, right by the water's edge.

"Where did he go, Taiga?" cried Ella. "Show me boy!"

Taiga only whined and sat down on his rump.

As Ella stared into the swamp water, her stomach sank. "He went in," she told Gran, who had come up beside her. "He went in to try his potion of water breathing!"

Gran's face looked pinched and drawn in the moonlight. "Dear Golem, I hope not," she whispered.

Her tone sent a trickle of fear running down Ella's spine. She whirled to face her grandmother. "Why not?" she said. "What's in there?"

"The Drowned!" It was Rowan who hollered the words. She was pacing along the shore, searching the dark waters herself.

Ella instantly pictured the Drowned—the zombies who lived at the bottom of the swamp. If Jack had swam anywhere near them, they might have reached up and grabbed him. They might have taken him to the bottom of the swamp too.

Before Ella even knew she had made the decision, she was stepping into the icy water.

"Ella, no!"

Gran grabbed for her hand to stop her, but Ella waved it away.

"My helmet is enchanted," she said, pulling it tightly over her head. "Enchanted with Respiration. I can breathe underwater, Gran. I can find Jack. I *will* find him!"

But as she dipped her face into the murky yellow water, she wondered, *Will I even be able to* see *him? Or will I run into a Drowned first?*

Then something tugged at the back of her chestplate. Ella came up out of the water flailing and hollering. "Gran, no!"

But it wasn't Gran who had pulled Ella back out. It was *Taiga*. Now the wolf was growling, tugging at Ella's leggings, trying to drag her back onto shore.

"Stop!" Ella cried. "Let me go!"

But the wolf wouldn't. And he won.

Ella tumbled back onto dry ground, with her wet wolf pressing his body against hers so that she wouldn't try to get back up.

Then Rowan let out a happy *whoop*, and waved at Ella and Gran from a few yards away.

"Jack's okay!" she cried. "He left us a sign. He *didn't* go into the water!"

She pointed toward a potion bottle resting on a rock.

Ella wrung out her shirt and hurried toward the

bottle, her water-logged boots squishing with every step.

The bottle was empty, but the cork was definitely Jack's. She could see the "J" etched onto its side, like a reassuring smile. And that bottle was pointing toward a trail.

"What a clever boy!" said Gran. "He knew we would come for him, and he marked a path for us."

Ella wouldn't believe it—not until Taiga sniffed the ground near the stone and took off running toward the trail.

Then her knees nearly gave way with relief. And though she was dripping wet from head to toe, a wave of warmth passed through her.

Jack hadn't drowned. Jack was okay. Jack was okay!

* * *

Ella knew they had entered the jungle before anyone said so. The trees were thick with vines and clusters of cocoa beans. Grasses grew taller, bushes grew thicker, and a damp heaviness hung in the air.

Beneath their feet, Jack's scent was tougher to track. Ella could tell, because Taiga led them in circles, around and around a small jungle pond.

More water, she realized, wondering again if Jack had gone in.

Then she had another thought. Maybe he hadn't gone *swimming*. Maybe he'd gone fishing!

"Jack was circling the pond too," she announced. "Looking for the perfect place to cast his line!"

The thought made her smile. It meant Jack had come this far. And hopefully he had found food.

Not far from the pond, Gran spotted something else. She called Rowan and Ella over to take a look.

"What is it?" asked Ella, peering through the vines at a cluster of twigs, leaves, and branches.

"Shelter," said Gran. "Your cousin knew enough to build himself a shelter for protection."

It's sure not much of one, Ella thought to herself. If she blew hard, she was pretty sure those branches would topple over. "How do you know it was his?" she asked.

Gran pointed to the vines wrapped around the tree overhead. A potion bottle, with a cork marked "J," was tucked tenderly into the net of vines.

Ella smiled. Then she peered into what looked like the front door. She half expected to find Jack in there, curled up asleep, with his stomach full of fish. But the shelter was empty.

She slid the potion bottle from the web of vines and tucked it into her backpack. Ella didn't want to leave any piece of Jack behind—not a single one.

As a breeze rippled through the branches overhead, she shivered. Her clothes had finally dried, but she couldn't help remembering the witch, the sound of glass breaking, and the witch's satisfied cackle as she disappeared back into her hut.

What mobs would they face here in the jungle?

When Gran answered, Ella realized she'd asked the question out loud. "Spiders, skeletons, creepers, zombies. Be prepared for anything," said Gran. She shaded her eyes and looked up, as if a spider might be poised overhead, ready to drop down.

"And ocelots?" asked Rowan.

The question jogged Ella's memory. *An ocelot might be hurt,* Jack had written in his note. But how did he know? Had an ocelot called to him?

"Ocelots too," said Gran thoughtfully. "But that's a critter, not a mob. If you see one, just stand still—it won't hurt you."

Ella's eyes slid across the bushes, searching for the spotted yellow coat of a wild cat. Was one watching them now? Would she see its green eyes staring at her? Or catch the flick of its tail in the brush of the jungle? Would it *growl* at her?

When a loud *hiss* rose from the bushes, Ella jumped backward.

And began to run.

CHAPTER 6

"**E**lla!" cried Rowan. "Stop!"

It was the laughter in her voice that made Ella pause. Rowan didn't sound frightened. She sounded . . . amused.

Slowly, with Taiga glued to her side, Ella followed the trail back toward Gran and Rowan. She searched the bushes for the hissing mob, but saw nothing. "Where's the creeper?" she asked.

"Here," said Gran softly. She pointed up, to a low-hanging tree limb. But it wasn't a creeper sitting on the branch. It was a bright red *parrot*.

As Gran looked up, the parrot looked down. And then, as if Gran had extended an invitation, the parrot flapped its wings and flew down to Gran's shoulder. When she turned to face the bird, it pecked gently at her nose, like a kiss. Then it bobbed its head, doing a little dance.

Ella giggled—and clamped her hand over her mouth. She didn't want to scare the bird away!

Then she remembered. "I heard a creeper," she said. "I know I did!" She looked again at the bushes, watching for any sign of movement.

"You heard a parrot *imitating* a creeper," said Gran, grinning.

As her shoulders shook with laughter, the bird hung on tight. And then, as if to prove Gran's point, he let out a low *hiss*. Two *hisses,* in fact. Then he pointed his beak toward a bush and bobbed his head, hissing again.

Ella's gaze drifted toward the bush. *Maybe he's not only imitating a creeper,* she thought. *Maybe he's warning us of one!*

Sure enough, a deadly *hiss* emerged from the bush.

The bird squawked, flapped its wings, and took off for the trees.

"Creeper!" cried Rowan, grabbing her bow.

Taiga took off toward the bush, ready to take on the creeper himself.

"No!" cried Ella. "Come back!"

Just as the wolf-dog reached the foliage, the creeper blew. Gunpowder floated down like snowflakes. And Taiga tumbled backward.

Ella ran to him, stroking his fur. "Are you hurt, buddy?" she cried.

He whimpered, but he raised his head and gave her a wet lick. Then he climbed to his feet, tucking his tail between his legs.

When he trotted over to Gran, as if trying to get

away from the bush that had just exploded, Ella knew he was okay.

"Oh, buddy," she said. "You can't get that close to a creeper. You have to let Rowan take care of those mobs with her bow and arrow. Okay?"

He licked his snout, as if embarrassed at his own mistake.

Then Ella remembered the parrot. Where had it gone? As she looked up, into the tangled branches over Gran's head, Ella sucked in her breath. The tree canopy was dotted with splotches of color—reds, blues, greens, and grays. And those "splotches" were moving.

Parrots! A whole flock of them seemed to have settled into the tree.

They chirped and chattered, gazing down at Gran. Were they curious about her? Or adoring her, the way Taiga looked at Ella sometimes?

Rowan's jaw dropped too. "What's going on?" she asked, pointing.

Gran shrugged, but she was smiling. "It seems as if I've made a few friends."

Something about her smile made Ella wonder: *Is Gran talking to these birds, the way she can talk to horses? Did she call them here?*

Gran wouldn't say so. But as they walked on through the jungle, Ella heard the rustle in the branches behind them. The parrots were following!

Taiga paced the trail below, barking up at the birds.

"No, Taiga—find Jack's scent," Ella told him. "Where's Jack?"

Her wolf-dog obeyed, dropping his nose back down to the ground. But once again, the trail stopped at water. When they reached a jungle stream, Taiga barked. And sat down.

Ella did, too, dropping her face into her hands. She couldn't shake the feeling that somehow, Jack had entered a body of water—and gotten into trouble.

"Why would he walk straight into a river?" she finally asked Gran.

Gran's face tightened. "Maybe he was fending off a mob," she said. "Going into the water might have been the smartest thing Jack could do. Mobs can't spawn in water. And most mobs take damage from water, right?"

Ella nodded. Gran had a point there. *But little boys can take damage from water too,* she thought to herself.

Rowan paced alongside the river, looking every bit as nervous as Ella felt.

"Jack mentioned a jungle temple in his note," Rowan said. "So where is the temple? Where do we find one?" She threw up her hands, as if she'd just asked a question that no one in the Overworld could answer.

The parrots twittered overhead. There was a great fluttering of wings, and then a bright red feather drifted down from the branches. Gran plucked it off the ground and stuck it behind her ear.

"I think I know where to find the temple," she said with a secret smile. "Follow me."

* * *

They walked upstream for what felt like hours. Ella's feet throbbed with each step, blistering within the boots that only a short while ago had been filled with swamp water.

The sun was up now, though Ella could barely see it through the thick canopy of the jungle—and through the flock of parrots that hovered overhead, like a patchwork tent or brightly colored umbrella.

Gran took long, steady strides. She knew exactly where she was going, with that red feather tucked behind her ear.

The parrots told her where to find the temple, Ella realized. She was sure of it now!

But for some reason, Gran wouldn't speak of it. Maybe she'd learned not to during the Uprising, when the villagers had turned against her because of her special gift. Because she—along with Ella, Jack, and Rowan's parents—had led great armies of animals against the hostile mobs that were spawning across the Overworld.

So why weren't the villagers grateful? Ella wanted to know. *Grateful to Gran for saving them?* Anger formed in the pit of her chest, like a mob spawner filled with flames.

But as they rounded a bend in the stream and jogged down a short hill, Ella saw something that extinguished those flames—like a bucket of cold water.

What she saw was a village—a *jungle* village—made up entirely of tree houses built high above the jungle floor.

Only these weren't crude shelters like what Jack had built. These were real homes, with two or three floors. With windows and doors. With rope bridges strung between them like inviting walkways.

Vine ladders led down to the ground below. Ella hurried toward the nearest one. She could hardly wait to climb up—to see what the jungle village looked like from above!

"Ella!"

Gran's voice was sharp as an arrow.

When Ella turned to face her, she saw something etched into Gran's face. She saw *fear*. But why?

"Why can't we just take a look?" pleaded Rowan.

Gran shook her head. "I told you. We're staying out of villages. We don't have time."

Ella caught Rowan's eye, and saw the question mark there.

What was Gran so afraid of?

And *how* could they avoid the village? The only way around it was to cross the stream, which was more like a roaring river now. Ella watched Gran's eyes flicker first to the river, and then to the village, and then back again.

Moments passed in silence, except for the parrots twittering overhead. Were they talking to Gran? Was she *listening* anymore?

Then Ella heard a low growl.

Taiga stiffened beside her, his nose pointed toward the base of the nearest tree. When she felt the fur rise on his back, she jumped up.

"What?" she whispered, reaching for her sword.

She saw a flash of movement, a streak of spotted fur.

Then an ocelot sprang out from behind the jungle tree.

CHAPTER 7

The cat landed on a boulder beside the river's edge. Taiga tore after her, his claws scrabbling against the boulder. He barked wildly, trying to reach her, while the ocelot growled and swiped at him from up above.

"Ella, get ahold of your wolf!" Gran hollered. "Taiga, *sit!*"

It wasn't until Ella said it that Taiga obeyed—and even then, he let out a terrible whine.

But Ella kept ahold of him, just as Gran had said. Just long enough for the ocelot to stop growling and to settle onto the boulder, safely above.

Gran spoke softly, taking slow steps toward the cat. Was she talking to her?

If she was, the animal wasn't listening. Her eyes were still locked with Taiga's. The two were at a stand-still, and Ella wasn't sure which animal would win.

"Who has fish?" Gran asked, waving her behind her. "Find some for me, quickly."

Both girls dropped to their knees and unzipped their packs. Ella found a loaf of bread, which was much smaller now than when they had started. And a bag of apples from the trees that grew outside Gran's mansion.

As she caught a whiff of the red apples, Ella suddenly felt homesick. She closed her eyes and imagined that they were all back at Gran's right now—even Jack. That he was out fishing in the courtyard, without a care in the world.

But we're not, Ella remembered. *We're in the middle of the jungle, with a wild ocelot—and no jungle temple in sight.*

Rowan pulled a wrapped package from her bag. "Dried fish!" she called out. She reached into the package and broke off a hunk.

Gran took a step or two backward, just enough to reach the fish. Then she slowly held it out toward the ocelot.

The spotted cat lifted its head from the rock and sniffed. Her nose and whiskers twitched. But she wouldn't come to Gran—no matter how much Gran tried to coax her.

Instead, she got up from the rock and started to pace. She let out a pitiful cry, and then she climbed down the rocks.

Taiga strained at Ella's side, wanting to break free. But Ella wouldn't let him.

As the ocelot leaped off the last rock, Ella noticed something sticking out of her side.

Was it a bone? A piece of wood? No.

It's an arrow! Ella suddenly realized. A broken arrow—as if the cat had been wounded and then had healed, with the arrow still embedded in its side.

"It's hurt!" cried Ella. She tried to show Gran, but the ocelot turned away too quickly.

Then Ella remembered Jack's note. *An ocelot might be hurt.* "It's Jack's ocelot!" she cried, causing Taiga to start barking all over again.

Rowan's eyes widened—she remembered the note too.

"It's Jack's ocelot," said Gran, nodding, as if everything suddenly made sense. "That's why she wouldn't let me tame her. She already belongs to someone else."

Ella pictured Jack, taming the ocelot with a piece of fish, maybe even the salmon he had been fishing for back at Gran's pond. *I scolded him for that,* she remembered. *But was he fishing for his ocelot? Had the cat already called to him for help?*

"Come back," she whispered to the ocelot, wishing she could remove the arrow and heal the beautiful animal.

But the ocelot wouldn't come back. Instead, she took a few steps in the other direction—toward the jungle village. Then she turned and let out a pitiful mew, as if she wanted them to follow.

"She's leading us to Jack," said Ella. "We have to follow her!"

But following her would mean walking straight into the village. Would Gran go?

The cat cried out three times, each more gut-wrenching than the first. But Gran stood firmly beside the river, until the parrots began to squawk overhead. Then finally, Gran took a stilted step forward, as if she'd had to uproot her foot from the earth.

"Let's go," she said to the girls. "Let's go find Jack."

But her face was white as snow.

*   *   *

The ocelot led them beneath the jungle village, around tree trunks and beneath vine ladders.

All the while, Ella kept one hand on Taiga's scruff—and her eyes trained up. What a magical place! When she heard giggling, she glanced over her shoulder—and saw a villager child swinging from a rope.

But where were all the grown-ups?

The cat led them onward, toward what looked like a village well. There, Ella saw some sort of market. A farmer pushed a cart full of cocoa beans. Another displayed fresh fish on a log table.

"Maybe Jack was here," said Rowan. "Maybe he made a trade!"

Ella waited for Gran to approach one of the farmers. But when she turned around, she saw that her grandmother was practically hidden behind a mass of vines.

Luckily, Rowan wasn't afraid to speak to grown-ups.

"We're looking for a boy," she said to the cocoa bean farmer. "About this high, with dark hair, wearing a red sweatshirt."

Dark messy *hair,* Ella wanted to add, but she suddenly couldn't find her voice.

The farmer nodded. "He was here," he said. "Trading fish for a map, I think. Check with the cartographer, if you'd like." He pointed toward the library.

Rowan thanked him and hurried toward the library. Ella followed, but Gran stayed hidden in the trees. As Ella glanced back, she saw that Gran's flock of parrots had grown. Birds of every color clustered overhead—so many of them that the villagers had begun to notice.

The fisherman quickly covered his fish, as if he feared the birds would eat them. Then he called out to Ella. "Hey, girl," he called. "You, there! Come here."

Ella fought the urge to run.

When he called out again in his gruff voice, Taiga growled—and Gran was suddenly by Ella's side.

"What do you want with the girl?" she asked sharply.

The fisherman's face darkened. But when he turned toward Gran, his jaw dropped open.

Gran's parrots had flown out of the tree. They perched along the well, on the farmer's cart, and on the ground beside Gran's feet—anywhere to be close to her.

To protect her? Ella wondered. *And me?*

The fisherman staggered backward, leaving his fish behind. Then he took off running.

Soon, a low murmur spread throughout the jungle

village. Faces lined the rope bridges overhead. Men and women spilled out onto the decks of their treehouses to see the birds below.

"Come on," urged Gran, pulling Ella away from the market.

But Rowan was still in the library! And where had Jack's ocelot gone?

"Wait!" cried Ella. "We can't leave Rowan!"

"We *have* to," said Gran, so sternly that Ella's breath caught in her chest.

Now the villagers were spilling down from the trees, climbing ladders and swinging from ropes. They were pointing and whispering. And some had begun to shout out.

Above the buzz of the crowd, Ella heard the *yowl* of the ocelot.

Then she heard something else. She heard a villager holler above the crowd.

"It's the witch! The witch who speaks to animals!"

CHAPTER 8

Ella stumbled, tripping over tree roots as Gran pulled her back into the safety of the jungle. Then she realized Taiga wasn't with her. He had stayed behind, snarling and snapping at the suddenly angry crowd.

"Taiga, come!" cried Ella.

He barked and then tore after her into the woods.

But where was Rowan? *We can't leave her behind!* thought Ella, squeezing back hot tears.

Finally, Gran stopped running. Because there was nowhere else to run. They'd reached the edge of the stream. Again.

Gran teetered there, as if she might jump into the roaring water. As if it might beat the alternative—facing the crowd of villagers who thought she was a witch.

But then Gran closed her eyes and took a deep breath. And Ella saw her transform back into the grandmother she knew—the one who would never, *ever* leave Rowan behind.

"Ella," she said, sinking down onto a stone. "This is what's going to happen."

Those six words turned Ella's blood to ice. "No, Gran," she said, not wanting to hear whatever was coming next.

"Listen!" Gran reached out and squeezed her hands. "The villagers are going to come for me. And I'm going to let them."

"No!"

"*Yes.* Ella, listen. You need to find Rowan. And then you need to leave—leave the jungle village. Follow Jack's ocelot, but be sure Taiga doesn't scare her away. You'll need that cat, do you understand? She'll lead you to Jack."

Ella nodded, but tears were spilling down her cheeks.

Gran pulled her into a tight hug. Then she pushed her away. "Ella, go," she said. "Take Taiga and go."

Ella took one last look at her grandmother, who looked strong as a statue standing beside that river. Like an iron golem, guarding her home—or her grandchildren. She no longer looked scared. She looked stoic. Strong. Unbreakable.

I hope she is, thought Ella. *Please be okay, Gran. Please be okay!*

It wasn't until Ella had followed Taiga halfway back to the village that a new worry flooded her mind.

Will we *be okay?* she wondered. *How can we go on without Gran?*

She raced along the jungle path, eager to find Rowan. Because Rowan was a warrior. Rowan would know what to do.

Unless, thought Ella with horror, *the villagers have taken Rowan too!*

*   *   *

Snap!

A twig broke beneath Ella's foot. She held her breath, wondering if the villagers had heard.

She'd made it back to the market now. Even Taiga seemed to be tiptoeing, his ears pricked forward and his eyes trained on the cluster of people surrounding the well.

Was Rowan one of them? Ella strained her eyes to see. Where had her cousin gone?

A stray parrot sat on the well. Then Ella saw the fisherman approach—raising his bow and arrow.

"No!" Ella cried out without thinking. "Don't hurt Gran's bird!"

But someone else had hollered too.

Then Ella saw Rowan—fierce Rowan—sprinting across the market with her trident in hand. Before the fisherman could fire an arrow, Rowan had knocked the bow out of his hands with her trident.

He stared at her in shock, and then anger. "Get the girl!" he hollered, pointing.

Ella saw the villagers snap to attention. She could feel the heat of the mob—the villagers who thought that Gran was evil. That the parrots were evil. And now, that Rowan was evil, too, for trying to protect the birds.

"Rowan!" Ella cried from her hiding place in the woods. "Here!"

Rowan's head whirled around. When she caught sight of Ella, she flew toward her, nearly knocking her over. "C'mon!" Rowan cried.

Ella grabbed her backpack and followed as fast as she could—hoping that she'd be fast enough.

Taiga barked as he tore through the jungle beside them.

Ella was running for her life right now, and Taiga seemed to know it. He was going to be there with her every step of the way.

* * *

"Rowan, stop!" Ella cried. She couldn't sprint anymore. She could barely even breathe.

She sank to the ground hoping to rest, if only for a few seconds.

"Not there!" hollered Rowan. "Here—we have to hide." She pulled Ella backward toward a bush.

Ella climbed under the cover of the tangled leaves and vines, and Rowan followed. Taiga sat panting in front of the bush, as if standing guard.

When Ella had finally caught her breath, she looked over at her cousin. Rowan's red hair hung loose from her ponytail. Dirt was smeared across her cheek. And her green eyes had never looked so wild.

Rowan met her gaze. "Where's Gran?" she asked.

Ella started to cry—she couldn't help it! Her chest heaved once, and then twice, before she could speak. "They took her," she said. "The villagers. They think she's a witch, because of the parrots."

Rowan's face turned to stone. "We have to go back for her," she said, pushing up off the ground.

"No! Gran said not to. She said we have to find Jack. His ocelot will show us the way."

Rowan scoffed. "What ocelot? I don't see one, do you?"

Ella peered through the thicket. They'd been running for fifteen minutes now—straight through the jungle. They'd left the ocelot behind long ago, she suddenly realized.

"Maybe Taiga could find her," she said, thinking out loud.

"No. He'd scare her away," said Rowan.

Maybe so, thought Ella. Having Taiga track the ocelot wasn't the best idea. But what choice did they have? They couldn't go back into the village for a map, or to ask someone for help. They might be snatched up by the villagers, just like Gran!

"Taiga can do it," she said, more firmly this time.

He whined from outside the shelter, cocking his head as if to say, *Do what?*

"Find the ocelot," she whispered, reaching through the branches to scratch his head. *Find Jack's ocelot. But don't hurt her! And don't scare her away. Promise me, buddy. We need you.*

He gazed back at Ella, his golden eyes so wise and full of warmth that she wanted to cry all over again. He wanted to help her, she could tell. That's all Taiga *ever* wanted to do.

He barked with excitement and jumped to his feet.

As they left the shelter of the leaves, Rowan was still mumbling. "It's a bad idea," she kept saying.

But Ella ignored her.

I trust my wolf, she thought to herself. *He won't let me down.*

* * *

Darkness was falling again. Ella could feel it more than see it. She shivered and quickened her pace.

Up ahead, Taiga sniffed the ground. The leaves. The trees.

"Will he ever stop?" asked Rowan from behind.

Ella turned, surprised to see her cousin so tired. Usually Rowan was in the lead. Rowan was the fighter, eager to press on ahead. But now, she looked defeated.

So I have to take charge, Ella realized.

"He'll stop soon," she said. "The ocelot couldn't have gone far. We'll find her soon."

Rowan heaved an enormous sigh, as if to say, "I'll believe it when I see it."

That's when Taiga growled.

Ella froze, keeping her body still as her eyes scanned the trees and bushes ahead.

"Where is she, buddy?" she asked her wolf.

He growled again and began pawing the base of a jungle tree.

Ella raised her eyes slowly, not wanting to startle the ocelot.

But as her gaze traveled up, up, up, it finally stopped—and she found herself staring straight into the glowing red eyes of an enormous spider.

CHAPTER 9

The spider let out a slow *hiss*. Then, before Ella could move, it scuttled forward, crawling down the trunk of the tree.

Grab your sword, Ella told herself. *Do it! Now!*

But she was frozen.

The spider crept closer, its fuzzy limbs reaching toward her through the darkness of the night.

Taiga snapped and snarled, trying to climb the base of the tree—to get to the spider before the spider got to Ella.

But something got to it first.

An *ocelot.*

As she leaped from a higher branch, she knocked the spider from its perch. The fuzzy mob hit the ground with an ear-piercing *squeal.*

It scuttled sideways, its red eyes trained on the wild cat. But the ocelot sprang again, snarling. She swiped at the spider with her claws, lifting it from the ground and sending it sailing into the thicket.

Ella heard the crunching of leaves and twigs as the spider scurried away. And then she fell to her knees.

The ocelot leaped up onto a rock, staring down at Ella.

"You did it, girl," said Ella. "Did you do it for me—or for Jack?"

Taiga whined and wiggled his body between Ella and the ocelot, as if to say, *She's mine!*

"It's okay," said Ella, hugging him close. "I'm yours. This cat belongs to Jack. But we owe her a thank you, don't we?"

"How do you know it's Jack's ocelot?" asked Rowan as she crept up behind Ella.

"I know," said Ella. "See the arrow stuck in her fur?"

As soon as Ella had a firm hold on Taiga, the cat began to slowly, carefully, climb down from the rock. With each step, the broken arrow bobbed side to side. Sure enough, this was Jack's ocelot.

Poor thing, thought Ella, wishing again that she could help.

But the cat wouldn't let her come near. Instead, it began its game of Follow the Leader again, leading them down the trail and then checking back to be sure they were following.

Ella felt Taiga relax beneath her hand. *He won't scare the ocelot,* she knew. *Because I asked him not to.*

Sure enough, as she released her hand, he stayed in step with her, never running too far ahead.

The four of them moved through the jungle, slowly at first. But when the ocelot saw that the others were following, she quickened her pace—slipping through bushes and around tree trunks. Ella and Rowan had to jog to keep up, holding their torch high to light the trail.

Ella fought back sleep, trying to stay alert. She listened for mobs. She searched the bushes, too, for glowing eyes or the gleam of a skeleton bone.

When a branch slapped against her face, she cried out—startled. But as she pushed her way through the thick brambles, she saw something.

A tower of moss-covered cobblestone rose before her.

The temple!

It was lit by torches, as if someone had been there recently—or still was. Was it two stories high? Or three? Ella marveled at the building, which was so covered in moss and vines that she might not have even seen it, if the ocelot hadn't led her straight to it.

Rowan was already running toward the temple, and Taiga whined, wanting to run too.

"Rowan, wait!"

Ella couldn't see an entrance. And where had the ocelot gone? She searched the ground, and then the trees above.

There! The wild cat had climbed a tree that stretched out over the temple. She crept out along a low branch, and there she sat, gazing down—as if to say, *This is as far as I go.*

Ella took a deep breath. "Okay, Taiga, let's go," she said.

The wolf-dog took off like a shot.

They followed Rowan round and round the base of the temple, searching for an opening. When Ella passed a torch, she reached up to grab it to help light the way.

Finally, she heard Rowan call to her.

Rowan was kneeling on a stone, pointing at something. There, nestled against a patch of moss, was an empty potion bottle. The neck of the bottle led them toward a dark, gaping entrance nearly hidden within the maze of cobblestone walls.

"Jack's showing us the way!" Ella cried.

The entrance led them down a mossy corridor. Ella pushed her way through a curtain of vines and then followed Rowan toward a staircase. One set of stairs led up. The other led down.

Ella shivered, imagining a dank basement like the one at Gran's house. "Let's go up," she said.

She was surprised when Rowan let her take the lead.

Taiga followed them up the stairs, sticking close to Ella's side. But the upper level of the temple revealed nothing but windows. The moon was rising once again over the jungle, casting dark shadows over the carpet of vines below.

"Slow down to appreciate one beautiful thing every day," Ella said out loud. It's something Gran liked to say.

But as she locked eyes with Rowan, Ella felt a lump rise in her throat.

Gran's not here to enjoy it, she remembered. *And there's no time to slow down now.*

Rowan hurried back down the staircase, and then around the bend toward the second set of stairs. "Jack!" she called out, as if their cousin would suddenly appear in the middle of this tower of stone.

Ella followed quickly, trying to keep up. She slipped on the second to last step and tumbled into Rowan's back.

As Rowan held out one arm to steady her, she pointed with the other. "What are those?"

Ella glanced over her shoulder. Three large levers protruded from the stone. "I don't know," she said. "But don't touch them, okay?"

Too late. Rowan was already playing with the levers, pulling one down and then another. When nothing happened, she lost patience and started down another hall.

"It's too dark," called Ella. "Take the torch!"

But as soon as Rowan did, Ella wished she hadn't given it up. She had to feel her way down the cobblestone hallway, just to be sure she didn't trip.

Then Rowan shrieked from the end of the hall, sending a redstone current down Ella's spine.

As Ella raced to her side, she saw it too—something that brought her to tears. Rowan was holding a backpack.

Jack's backpack.

As she gave it a gentle shake, they heard the *tink-tink* of potions inside.

"Jack would never leave those behind!" Ella cried. "Jack! Where are you?"

She convinced herself for a brief moment that he was standing right next to her—that he had guzzled a potion of invisibility and was just playing a trick.

But as she waved her arm around, calling his name, she knew with certainty. Jack wasn't here. Something had happened to Jack!

Ella grabbed the torch from Rowan's hand and swung it around the room, hoping to find a clue. Another hallway stretched into darkness. As Ella started down it, Taiga barked a warning. He took off, brushing past Ella so that he would be first.

First to set off the tripwire.

It's a trap! Ella realized—too late.

As she watched in horror, the wall opened up, releasing a barrage of arrows.

Thwack, thwack, thwack!

As she dropped the torch in surprise, the room went dark.

And Taiga let out a piercing yelp.

CHAPTER 10

Rowan scooped the torch from the floor just as Ella reached Taiga. In the dim light, she saw him lick his fur. She felt the warm blood.

"He's hurt!" she cried. She gathered the hem of her cape in her hands and pressed it against Taiga's side, hoping to stop the bleeding.

Rowan stepped closer with the torch. "Let me see," she said. "Was it an arrow?"

When Ella took the cloth away, she could see the wound in the light. It was bleeding, but it wasn't deep.

"He was only grazed," said Rowan, blowing out her breath.

Ella buried her face in Taiga's fur, whispering a thank you to the universe. She thought of the ocelot outside, with the broken arrow in her side. Had she set off the tripwire too? Is that how she'd gotten hurt?

As Ella pulled Taiga into her arms, the temple

around her felt darker somehow, and dangerous—as if more traps and tripwires were waiting around every corner.

"Let's get out of here," she said to Rowan. "Jack's not here."

Rowan nodded.

They hurried up the steps and back out the entrance. But as the chilly night air hit Ella's face, she heard something.

A *hiss*. And then a *yowl*. The ocelot dropped from the tree branch down to the ground, blocking Ella's path.

When Ella jumped backward in surprise, Taiga began to growl.

"No, hush!" cried Ella, reaching down to quiet her dog. But her own skin prickled with fear. Why was the ocelot hissing at her?

She stared into the animal's eyes, wishing she could communicate with her the way she did with her wolf. "What is it?" she asked the wild cat. "What do you want me to do?"

The cat *yowled* again and began to pace. She stepped toward the temple, and then away again.

"She wants us to go back inside," said Rowan. "We missed something."

Ella shivered. She didn't *want* to go back inside. Taiga had been hurt, trying to protect her. What would happen next?

She dropped down beside her wolf and checked his side again. The bleeding had stopped, but he shrank away from her hand, as if the site of the wound were still tender.

"What do we do?" Ella asked Taiga.

He barked once, as if to say, "Go. Follow her. Find Jack!"

Taiga is a warrior, like Rowan, Ella thought again. *And I have to be too.*

As she followed the bobbing light of Rowan's torch back into the temple, Ella called out. "Jack! Are you here? Help us find you!"

At first, she heard nothing.

But then, in the stillness of the night, she heard a faint sound, like the *mew* of a cat. Had the ocelot followed them?

She heard the sound again. It wasn't a cat at all. It was human, like the cry of a small child. Or . . .

"Jack!"

He responded, louder this time. "I'm here!" But where was it coming from? Down below?

Ella began patting the floor with her hands. Rowan held the torch high so that they could search for cracks in the stones. Even Taiga sniffed the cobblestone, scratching at it with his paws.

"Where are you?" Ella called, over and over again.

Every time Jack answered, they moved a little closer to the sound of his voice. Until Ella was quite sure that Jack was nearby—just a few feet below them. She pressed her ear to the stone and asked him again, "Where are you?"

"In the treasure room!" he cried.

The treasure room?

"We have to solve the puzzle—the one with the levers," cried Rowan, smacking her fist into her hand. "I knew it!"

"But you don't know how," said Ella.

Then she heard another peep from below. "I do!"

Of course, Jack knew. That's how he had gotten into the treasure room to begin with!

"Tell us, Jack," she cried. "Tell us how!"

As he called out instructions to Ella, she relayed them to Rowan, who had headed back downstairs to the wall with the levers.

"Flip the lever farthest away from the stairs."

"Got it!" Rowan shouted.

"Good. Now flip the lever closest to the stairs."

"Done," Rowan announced.

"Okay, now put them back where they started," said Ella. "Wait! Do it in the right order! Flip the lever closest to the stairs. Now flip the lever furthest from the stairs."

"Back where they started?" scoffed Rowan. "That can't be right!"

Except it was.

Because Ella suddenly heard a deafening *click*. The stone beneath her hands began to slide open. She sprang backward so that she wouldn't fall down into the tiny room below . . .

. . . where Jack's flushed face was looking up.

"Jack!"

Ella slid down through the trapdoor until she was

standing beside him. She hugged him close. "Are you okay?" She pushed him away so that she could check him from head to toe, as if he were her wolf-dog and had just set off a tripwire.

"I'm alright," he grumbled, pulling himself free.

Rowan's face suddenly appeared in the hole above. "Jack!" she half-cried, half-scolded. "Do you know how long we've been looking for you?"

She climbed down through the trapdoor until she was standing on the lid of the chest below. "How could you leave like that?" she said. "In the middle of the night?"

Jack set his jaw and said simply, "My mother told me to. In her journal." He pointed toward the back-pack that Rowan had slung over her shoulder.

When she handed it to him, he dug through it—and came back up holding a worn leather book. As he flipped through the pages, Ella caught glimpses of drawings and diagrams. Of potion brewing charts, and scrawled lists of ingredients.

Then he pulled out a scrap of paper and held it out for Ella to see.

Dearest Jack,

There will come a time when you will need to fight, just as I did. You'll need to fight with your potions—by gathering ingredients from all across the Overworld.

Gather as much as you can, dear boy. Because

*there will be another Uprising one day. I need you
to be ready—and brave. Don't wait too long. And
know your mother loves you.*

Mom

Ella's eyes brimmed with tears.

*What would it be like to get a message from my own
mother?* she wondered. *If she told me to take a journey
across the Overworld, would I do it?*

She didn't even have to think about it. *Yes,* she
knew. *I would.*

When Rowan read the note, her face softened too.
She wiped her nose and then straightened back up.

"But wait," said Ella, questions suddenly filling her
mind. "Your mother didn't mention the ocelot. Or the
temple. Or even the jungle. How did you . . . ?"

Jack's face spread into a slow smile. "My ocelot told
me," he said. "She brought me here." Then his face fell.
"She's hurt, though."

"I know," said Ella, squeezing his shoulder. "We
saw. She led us to you." She glanced up through the
trapdoor, wondering if the ocelot was still outside. Was
she waiting for Jack the way Taiga was waiting above
the trapdoor for her?

As if reading her mind, the wolf-dog barked.
He paced the cobblestone floor and stuck his snout
through the trapdoor opening, trying to lick her hand.

"It's okay, buddy," Ella called to him. "We'll be
right out."

Then Jack asked the question Ella had been dreading. "Where's Gran?"

Ella looked to Rowan, wondering how to tell him that Gran had been taken. That Gran was being held in the jungle, by villagers who thought she was a witch.

Rowan shook her head, as if to say, "Don't say a word."

But how can we not? Ella wondered. *I have to tell him something!*

She cleared her throat. But just as she opened her mouth to speak, she heard a *click.*

And the trapdoor above slid shut.

CHAPTER 11

"Let us out!"

As Rowan pounded on the trapdoor overhead, Ella heard Taiga barking wildly from up above. He wanted *into* the treasure room just as much as they wanted out.

"Did someone lock us in?" cried Ella. "Or did we just . . . wait too long?" She didn't know what to hope for. The thought of someone locking them in was terrifying. But if no one was up there—if the trapdoor had closed all on its own—then . . . who would get them out?

Rowan stopped pounding, as if she'd just had the same realization. She pulled her hand back to nurse her sore knuckles.

"Are we trapped again?" asked Jack, his voice rising with panic.

Ella sank down beside him. "It's okay," she said. "At least we're together now. We'll find our way out."

His face suddenly brightened. "Gran's out there! She'll save us!"

Ella looked away before Jack could spot the truth in her eyes. Gran *wasn't* out there. Gran was probably locked in a jail cell herself. *So we'll have to save ourselves,* thought Ella.

She began to search the room for weapons, tools— anything they could use to mine their way out. "Do you have your pickaxe?" she asked Jack.

He nodded and reached into his backpack.

When Rowan heard the question, she laid out her own weapons on the floor below. And Ella did too. Then they took stock.

One sword, enchanted with Fire Aspect.

One sword, enchanted with Smite.

A trident, with no enchantment at all.

And Jack's tiny pickaxe.

Ella sighed and reached for the pickaxe. It was the only thing here that *might* break through the cobble-stone wall.

She began tapping—first on one wall, and then the opposite wall. But both walls were solid stone. There was no way she could hack her way through!

"Let me try," said Rowan, reaching for the axe. But instead of hitting it against the wall, she whacked it against the dirt floor. And a hunk of dirt crumbled beneath their feet.

"That's it!" cried Ella. "That's our way out!"

Rowan struck the floor again and again, until she had tunneled a narrow path downward. Then she got on her hands and knees and began using the axe like a shovel, digging deeper.

When the bottom of the tunnel gave way, opening up to darkness, Rowan lurched forward—and braced herself with her hands just in time.

"Careful!" cried Ella.

Together, they watched the dirt tunnel collapse. The dirt and gravel fell away, and landed below with a *splash*.

Ella's stomach sank. She met Rowan's gaze.

They were above *water*, not land.

Which meant there was no way out.

* * *

"What are we waiting for?" asked Jack.

He'd been silent for so long, Ella thought he had given up. *Just like me,* she thought wearily.

But Jack pointed downward through the dirt tunnel. "What are we waiting for?" he asked again.

"It's *water*," said Ella. "Didn't you hear the splash? We don't know how deep it is, or how long we'd have to swim before we could come up for air."

"So?" said Jack with a shrug.

"So we'll *drown*," said Rowan, sounding exasperated.

"No we won't," said Jack. He reached deep into his backpack and sorted through a few glass bottles. When he pulled his hand back out, he held a vial of sea-blue potion. He splashed it side to side. "Potion of water breathing," he announced proudly.

"Jack!" Ella cried with relief. "You didn't use it yet?"

He cocked his head at her. "Why would I?" he asked. "I didn't need it until now."

Ella flushed warm with relief, and a twinge of guilt. She'd doubted Jack all along—believed he would do something foolish instead of saving his potion for just the right time.

But here he was, holding a full bottle of the very potion they needed most.

When Jack pulled the cork out, Ella quickly reached for the bottle. "Let me drink it," she said. As terrified as she was of dropping down a dirt tunnel into an unknown body of water, she was even *more* terrified of letting Jack do it.

But he tugged right back on the bottle. "It's *my* potion," he said. "I want to use it."

Ella looked to Rowan for help, but Jack had already made up his mind.

Rowan shrugged and pointed toward the helmet on Ella's head. "So go with him," she said.

Ella reached up and touched her leather helmet. She'd forgotten—with the Respiration enchantment, she *too* could breathe underwater! At least for a while.

She stared hard at Rowan. "Do you think it will work?" she asked. What she really wanted to ask was, *Will Jack and I survive this? Will we ever see you again?*

Rowan nodded—and forced a smile. "It'll work. But you two had better not forget about me in here, okay? You'd better come back for me!"

Jack grinned. "Okay. We will." Then he raised the

bottle, tilted his head back, and guzzled the blue liquid. He gave Ella a thumbs-up, and then he slid through the hole feet first.

When Ella heard the *splash* below, her stomach dropped. But there was no time to waste. Jack was down there all by himself—and she couldn't get to him fast enough.

She tightened her helmet, gave Rowan one last look, and then slid through the hole. As she broke free of the earth and began to fall, she heard Taiga bark from up above.

She had just enough time for a single thought: *I didn't say goodbye to Taiga!*

Then she hit the ice-cold water and plunged into darkness.

CHAPTER 12

Ella's lungs felt as if they would burst. She desperately needed to breathe!

Then she remembered—she *could* breathe, even underwater. Slowly at first, she inhaled through her nose, waiting to cough or choke. But she didn't. The water flowed into her lungs and back out again, as if she were a pufferfish in Gran's pond.

But this was no pond. This was a *river*.

And the current was so strong, Ella could barely swim. She gave over control and let the water take her, hoping she wouldn't crash into the wall—or go over some sort of falls.

As the current pulled her forward through the cave, she squinted into the dark water, searching for Jack. She wished for a speck of light—from a lit torch or glowstone or *anything* that would allow her to find Jack in the swirling water.

Suddenly, the rocky ceiling gave way, and Ella saw the moon through the rippling water overhead. She swam up, up, up until her head burst through the surface.

She spit out the water that had filled her lungs, and then took a breath of cool night air. "Jack!" she cried. "Where are you?"

"Over here!"

He was so close, she nearly ran right into him. He clung to a fallen tree that was strewn across the stream like a bridge.

"Hang on!" she cried, searching for her own handle or foothold on the tree trunk. But the current was so strong. It tugged on her legs, threatening to pull her under again. And the tree was so slippery. "Hang on!" she said again, but this time, she was talking to herself.

Then someone yanked on her cape, pulling her upward. "Rowan?" she cried, struggling to turn around.

No. It was *Taiga.* The wolf lifted her backward with his powerful jaws, just enough for her to climb up onto the fallen log.

"Good boy," she cried, nuzzling his wet fur. "Now help Jack!"

Together, they pulled Jack out of the swirling water. Then Ella helped him half-crawl, half-walk across the log toward shore.

Once they'd reached solid ground, Taiga licked Ella's face until she laughed, pushing him away. "Enough!" she said. "I missed you too."

Jack was already on his feet, heading toward the trees.

"Jack, wait!" cried Ella. "We need to go get Rowan!"

But Jack had dropped to his knees. He held out his hand.

For what? Ella wondered.

Then she saw the shadow of the ocelot, creeping toward Jack. She sniffed his outstretched hand and rubbed her head against it. Even from a few yards away, Ella could hear the loud *purr.*

So Jack had found his animal—finally! The ocelot had called to him, led Ella and Rowan to his side, and waited for him to be freed from the trap in the jungle temple.

Ella tiptoed across the grass and rested her hand on Jack's shoulder. "I'm going to get Rowan," she whispered, trying not to scare the ocelot. Then she turned and hurried toward the temple, with Taiga close behind.

The temple seemed darker now than before. A single torch lit the entrance. Ella hurried down the cobblestone steps, hoping she would remember how to solve the puzzle and open the trapdoor.

When she reached the wall of switches, she began flipping them, remembering Jack's instructions in her head.

Flip the lever farthest away from the stairs.

Now flip the lever closest to the stairs.

Okay, now reverse that—put them back where they started.

As she flipped the last lever, she held her breath.

Click! She heard the trapdoor slide open, and Rowan's cheer of relief.

Ella raced back up the stairs and found Rowan, standing on the chest in the treasure room and waving through the trapdoor above.

"Crawl out!" cried Ella. "Before the door closes again!"

But Rowan didn't. Instead, she squatted down and patted the chest she'd been standing on. "Do you know what this is?" she asked.

Ella shook her head.

"A *treasure* chest," said Rowan. She crossed her arms and grinned, as if she'd just discovered a brand-new biome in the Overworld.

Ella leaned down through the trapdoor, eager to see what was inside the chest. But time was running out. "The door will close, Rowan," she reminded her. "And I don't know if I'm strong enough to keep it open."

Rowan nodded. "Well, this is strong enough—for sure." She reached into the treasure chest and pulled out an iron ingot. "Wedge the trapdoor open with it," she said.

So Ella did.

Only then did she lower herself into the treasure room to see what else Rowan had found in the chest.

The first thing she saw were more iron ingots, stacked in a tidy row. And beneath them? A gold ingot, shining brightly in the light of the torch.

"The gold one's mine!" Jack suddenly cried from above. "I found that! I'm bringing it home to make glistering melon for potions."

Rowan laughed. "Alright, alright," she said. "Finders keepers." But as she dug deeper, she found more treasures.

"Is that a skeleton bone?" asked Ella. She pulled it from the chest with her fingertips.

From up above, Taiga began to whine and drool.

"Yes, you can have it, buddy," said Ella, handing it up to her dog. "No one's going to fight you for that slimy old thing."

Then Rowan pulled out the most amazing treasure of all. A *book*. But it wasn't just any book.

In the darkness of the room, Ella caught the faint purple glow. It was an enchanted book! She reached for it and carefully opened its cover, inhaling the smell of dust—and possibility.

"Loyalty," she whispered, as soon as she recognized the enchantment. "This is exactly what we needed, Rowan, to enchant your trident!"

She waited for Rowan to say something—to sound at least a wee bit excited. But Rowan had fallen silent. She was staring into the bottom of the chest.

"What is it?" asked Ella. "More bones?"

Rowan shook her head. She reached deep into the chest and lifted something out. Something large, and made of leather.

A horse saddle.

Rowan lowered her head and sniffed it, the way Ella had sniffed her book.

"You can't bring that home!" cried Jack. "It's too big!"

"No bigger than your ocelot," Rowan snapped. She hugged the saddle to her chest.

"But—" Jack began to protest.

"Shh," said Ella, raising her finger to her lips. "It's okay."

I have my wolf, she realized. *Jack has his ocelot. But Rowan is still waiting for her horse.*

And maybe this saddle was a step toward finding it.

"Let's get out of here," said Ella. "Before the iron ingot gives way." She helped Rowan gather all of their weapons. Their backpacks. And their newfound treasures.

When everything had been lifted out of the treasure room, Ella pulled the iron ingot from where it was braced.

Instantly, the treasure door slid shut.

"Let's go," said Rowan. "Gran's waiting for us."

CHAPTER 13

When Jack asked again where Gran was, Ella told him. "We have to save her, Jack," she said, keeping her voice steady. "We'll need all of your potions."

He nodded solemnly.

They were following Taiga through the darkness, retracing their steps back toward the jungle village. Overhead, branches crackled, as the ocelot leaped from tree to tree.

When Ella glanced over her shoulder, she saw Rowan dragging her feet. She had strapped her saddle over her backpack, and now she looked like a sea turtle on land—and was moving just as slowly.

Ella wondered again if bringing the saddle had been such a good idea. Maybe Jack had been right. It was so big! How could Rowan fight with that on her back?

But she said nothing. When Rowan had set her mind on something, there was no stopping her.

When Jack reached into his backpack and offered her potion of swiftness, to help her walk faster, she shook her head no. "I'm fine," she said as she huffed and puffed along.

That's when an arrow soared over her shoulder and landed with a *thunk* in the trunk of a tree.

"Run!" she cried.

Jack ran up—climbing a vine-covered tree to be with his ocelot.

Ella dove down, pulling Taiga under a patchwork net of vines and leaves. The wolf paced and whined, begging to be set free so he could attack the skeletons that were surely coming their way. But Ella wouldn't let him. "You won't take another arrow for me," she said firmly. "Taiga, sit!"

He whined pitifully, but he sat.

Through the net of green, Ella saw Rowan pull her bow and turn to fight. *Thwack, thwack, thwack!* She sent a series of arrows into the thicket.

Ella heard a *grunt* and the tinkle of skeleton bones.

Again, Taiga strained to break free of the leafy green fortress. "Taiga, no!" Ella cried. "I said *sit*!"

Then she reached for her own bow and cleared a hole in the vines. Her fingers felt sweaty as she loaded her first arrow.

Rowan was still firing, thanks to the bow that Ella had enchanted with Infinity. *Thwack, thwack, thwack!*

Her arrows will never run out, Ella remembered.

But she had forgotten the enchantment she had used with her own bow. Until she aimed at the skeleton that had just stepped onto the trail.

Thwack! Crack! Whoosh!

The skeleton went up in flames. And so did the bush next to him.

I enchanted this bow with Flame! Ella realized.

As she watched the fire spread from one bush to the next, terror spread within her chest. *Did I just start a forest fire?* she wondered. *Even here in the damp jungle?*

Then she remembered Jack. She sprang from her hiding place and searched the tree above. "Jack, come down!" she cried. "Fire!" She couldn't see him in the thick canopy of the trees. Where was he?

As the fire spread closer, Ella reached for Rowan's arm. "Let's go!" she cried. "Let's get out of here!"

But Rowan wouldn't leave her post. "You go!" she said. "Get Jack. I'll cover you."

"I can't find him!"

Ella could barely hear her own voice over the crackle and roar of the flames. If the skeletons were hiding in the trees, surely they would be running away too—or burning—wouldn't they?

But as Rowan waved one last time at Ella, urging her to get Jack and *go* already, something struck Rowan from behind. A skeleton arrow hit her square in the back. And she fell forward with a grunt.

Ella froze. "Rowan!"

Her cousin lay perfectly still.

No, no, no! thought Ella. *I can't do this without you!* She fought back the wave of panic rising within her.

As the flames flickered along the trail toward Rowan, Ella finally sprang into action. She grabbed Rowan's arms and pulled her forward. "Taiga, help me!" cried Ella.

With her wolf-dog's help, they pulled Rowan off the trail. But the skeleton who had launched the arrow was coming. Ella looked out of the bushes just long enough to see the glowing white bones of the undead mob—and to see Jack coming down the tree trunk, out of hiding.

"Jack, no! Go back!" Ella cried. But it was too late. Her cousin was in danger, and Rowan wasn't there to protect him.

So Ella did the only thing she could think to do. She grabbed the trident from Rowan's belt and charged the skeleton.

She swung the trident as if it were a sword—an incredibly heavy sword. The blow knocked the skeleton to its knees. But still the mob raised its bow. And now Ella was the one in the line of fire.

So she swung the trident again. And again. Until her arms ached and the bony mob dropped to the ground with a grunt and the tinkle of bones.

Then Taiga was beside her. Instead of lunging for one of those bones, he licked her hands and wagged his tail with relief.

But there was no time to celebrate.

The fire was spreading. And there was no hiding from its flames.

Ella reached back into the thicket, tugging on Rowan's arms—trying to drag her cousin out of harm's way. But Rowan's saddle was stuck in the brambles!

And the jungle was filling with smoke.

"Jack, help me!" cried Ella, trying not to cough. "Where are you?"

He answered her with the sound of breaking glass. A bottle whizzed past her and landed at her feet with a *crack*. And as the bubbles rose, she heard his voice from up above. "Splash potion of fire resistance!" he called.

Warmth spread through Ella's body—and it wasn't only the potion. *Jack's still with me,* she realized. *Jack and his potions.*

As she glanced back into the thicket, she saw something else. Rowan lifted her head, ever so slightly. And reached backward to feel the arrow that had struck her from behind.

"What happened?" she asked as she tugged the arrow from the thick leather of the saddle.

Ella answered with a wobbly voice. "Your saddle," she said. "That heavy, clunky saddle saved your life!"

Even as a smoky haze filled the air between them, Rowan smiled. "So let's go," she said. "Now!"

* * *

A gentle rain was falling. As Ella turned back in the direction of the temple, she no longer saw a plume of smoke rising into the air. That meant the fire was out. It *hadn't* spread. She blew out a breath of relief.

Taiga scrambled ahead of them on the trail, nose to the ground.

"We're getting close to the jungle village," Rowan whispered. "I can feel it."

Ella could too. She glanced up, expecting to see tree houses and vine ladders any moment now. She could hear the roar of the river nearby. And a red-winged parrot hopped along a low-hanging branch, as if to say, *You're back! Woot-woot! Follow me!*

But as the first tree house came into view, Ella held out her hand to stop her cousins. "We don't have a plan!" she whispered. "How are we going to save Gran?"

Rowan reached for her sword, but Ella shook her head. "There are too many villagers," she said. "We could never fight them all. And I don't want to hurt anyone. We just need to set Gran free and get out of here!"

Jack didn't reach for a weapon. He reached for something else—the potions in his backpack. When he pulled one out, Ella waited to hear which one he had chosen. "Potion of invisibility," he announced.

Clear liquid sloshed within the bottle, and Ella could see that there was plenty of it—enough for Jack, Rowan, and herself. *And maybe for Taiga too?* she wondered.

"Jack, you're a genius," she declared.

Rowan nodded. "It could work," she said thoughtfully. "But before we drink it, let's try to figure out where they're holding Gran. Save the potion for when we need it most."

As they wound their way through the trees, skirting the edge of the village, Ella happened to look up at the sky. And she suddenly realized that finding Gran *wouldn't* be very difficult.

"Follow the parrots," she said, pointing up.

A flock of birds in every color of the rainbow hovered over the village, resting on tree branches, flying overhead, and hopping along fences and walls. They hadn't left Gran behind. They had stayed, keeping watch.

"Follow the parrots," Rowan repeated.

The thickest cluster sat on the rooftop of what looked like a blacksmith's shop, near to the village well. The building was made mostly of stone, with a blazing furnace on the front porch.

"I'll bet Gran's inside," whispered Ella.

Taiga nudged her leg, as if to say, *I think so too.*

But as Jack pulled out the potion of invisibility, Ella wondered again, *Can we use it on Taiga too?*

Jack's ocelot was hidden in the trees above. But Taiga wouldn't hide—Taiga would want to fight. To protect Ella. *So I have to protect him too,* she decided.

"Jack, does your potion work on wolves?" she whispered.

He shrugged. "I think so. We can try." He began to pull the cork from the bottle.

"Not yet!" Rowan cried. "Wait till we're closer."

They crept as close to the building as they could without being seen. Villagers milled around the well. Most of them looked up, studying the parrots, as if wondering how to get rid of them.

As a buzz of anxious voices filled the air, Ella was grateful for the noise—and the distraction. If the villagers were looking skyward, it would be much easier to sneak by unnoticed.

Especially if we're invisible, she thought with a grin.

"It's time," Rowan finally whispered, reaching for the bottle. She took the first swig, and immediately began to disappear. Only her sword was visible now.

"I'm next," said Jack, reminding Ella that it was *his* potion.

"Okay, buddy," she said. "Bottom's up."

Soon, Jack was gone too—except for his backpack.

Ella reached for the bottle and brought it to her lips. But then she remembered Taiga. "We'll share this," she whispered to her wolf. "You have to drink it, okay? No matter how nasty it tastes."

She poured a small puddle of the potion into the palm of her hand and offered it to her dog.

He sniffed it, took a step backward, and looked away.

"Drink it!" Ella urged, moving her hand closer to him. "You have to!"

He finally lapped up the liquid obediently. Then he licked his snout, as if to show her that he'd taken every last drop.

"Good boy," said Ella, just as her wolf-dog disappeared. "Now it's my turn."

She tilted the bottle and drank the last of the liquid. It tasted slightly of carrots, and something else—something *nasty.* Ella nearly gagged, hoping she hadn't just eaten a spider's eye or some other gross ingredient from Jack's bag of tricks. *Ugh.*

But as she looked down, her arms and legs quickly began to disappear.

"We'll have to leave our bags," came Rowan's voice—from out of nowhere. "Take off your backpacks, or we'll be spotted."

They piled up their things and hid them behind a tree trunk, taking only the weapons they needed. Then two swords and a potion bottle began bobbing toward the well.

CHAPTER 14

As they slid through the door of the blacksmith shop, Ella held her sword steady at her side, trying not to bang into anything or make any noise.

But she bumped into Rowan over and over again. "Stop that!" her cousin whispered.

"I can't help it!" How can you avoid someone you can't even see?

Ella reached down again to be sure Taiga was still beside her. She felt his hot breath on her hand and a reassuring lick.

Was Jack here too? Ella spun in a careful circle, searching for some glimpse of him. When she saw a potion bottle hovering over a wooden chest, she smiled.

But don't you dare open that chest! she wanted to say to Jack.

Before she could, she heard footsteps on stairs, and

a villager entered the back of the room. From his black apron and the soot on his hands, Ella could tell he was the blacksmith.

But what was downstairs? Had he just gone to check on Gran?

A hand reached back to stop Ella from moving.

Don't worry, Rowan, she wanted to say. *I'm not walking—or talking. I'm barely breathing.*

They stood frozen until the blacksmith stepped onto the porch. Then Rowan's hand tugged Ella toward the back of the room. Toward the staircase. And hopefully toward Gran too.

The steps to the basement were cracked and crumbly. Ella took them one by one. But not Taiga. The wolf-dog brushed past her. Ella heard his claws *click, click, click* across the basement floor. Then she heard a whine. And a voice. An oh-*so*-familiar voice. *Gran!*

Now Ella couldn't move fast enough. She felt Jack nudging her back, urging her to get going. He must have heard Gran's voice too!

When they hit the base of the stairs, Ella could see the bars of a cage—a cell. A *jail* cell. The villagers had thrown Gran in jail!

When Ella caught sight of Gran's weary face, she nearly cried. Then she remembered that Gran couldn't see *her.* But somehow, Gran knew they were there. Maybe Taiga had greeted her with a lick between those dreadful iron bars.

Gran looked around the room, as if searching for their faces. Then she slowly raised a finger to her lips.

Was someone else here?

Ella quickly scanned the room. She saw no villagers, but she did see something glowing red along the wall. A redstone circuit led from the jail cell up to a lever. *The lever that will set Gran free!* Ella realized.

Rowan got to the lever first, as usual. She flipped it down with a *click*. And the bars of the jail cell opened with a *creak*.

Gran stepped out in a flash. Then she waved them toward her. "Shh!" she said. "We have to be quiet. Is the blacksmith still upstairs?"

Ella shook her head no, and then realized again that Gran couldn't see her. "He's outside," she whispered. "On the porch."

"Then we'll have to use the back door," said Gran. "And we'll have to stick together. Jack, are you here?"

"Yes!"

Gran's eyes fill with tears. "Good. Well done, Jack," she said. "We missed you."

Ella imagined Jack's face flushing with pride. But there was no time for happy reunions now. Because the parrots on the rooftop had started squawking.

"They're warning us!" said Gran. "We have to move quickly."

She led the way up the staircase, stopping at the top to glance carefully through the crack in the door. She pushed through it gently.

But instead of turning right to go into the blacksmith's shop, Gran turned left. The back door was ajar, and Ella could see a sliver of light shining through.

The sun was up. That meant no mobs would spawn. *But it also means that we'll be seen*, thought Ella. *Or at least Gran will!*

Her heart thudded in her ears as she followed Gran outside. They hugged the wall as they rounded the corner of the building toward the well.

More villagers had gathered now, as if summoned by the squawking of the parrots. The villagers seemed angry, or frightened—or maybe both. Some shook their fists at the birds. Others raised their swords or even their bows, threatening to send arrows into the sky.

"Oh, dear," whispered Gran. "We'll need to leave quickly—and take those birds with us." She waved the children on, away from the well and toward the gushing river.

But Ella glanced backward. "Our things!" she cried. There was no way they could get to their belongings now. They'd have to run straight through the crowd of villagers!

"My backpack," said Jack. "It has my potions—and all the ingredients I collected. I need my backpack!"

Gran started to shush him, but then Rowan started in too. "I'm not leaving without my saddle," she announced.

"Saddle?" Gran's forehead crinkled. "Oh, dear."

"We have to go back," said Ella. She took another look around the corner, wondering if the ocelot still stood guard over their belongings. Was the cat watching them now, from the trees above?

I hope so, thought Ella. *We need all the help we can get!*

Gran gave them permission to go. "But leave your weapons here," she said. "Don't carry anything that the villagers might see. Hurry!"

Ella and Rowan handed Gran their swords. But Jack's potion bottle hovered in the air.

"Jack, give it to Gran," Ella whispered.

For a moment, the bottle didn't move. Then it took off like a shot and disappeared around the corner. "Jack!" Ella cried.

She raced after him—or after the potion bottle.

They wound around the market, past the crowd of villagers who had gathered there, and past the well. Ella was breathing so hard, she feared someone would hear her. But the parrots overhead were too loud. And villagers were shouting now too.

"Ring the bell tower!" someone suggested. "That'll scare the birds away!"

"Use TNT!" said another.

Ella ran faster. If there was going to be an explosion here sometime soon, she wanted her wolf-dog—and the parrots—to be as far away as possible.

Was Taiga at her feet now? She couldn't be sure. There was no time to stop. No time to call to him.

When she reached the place where they had left their belongings, Ella was relieved to see that they were still there, hidden behind a fat tree trunk. And when she glanced up, the ocelot was there, too, pacing along the branch.

The ocelot gazed straight into Ella's eyes. *It sees me,* Ella realized. Yet when she looked down, her arms and legs were still invisible. *So how does it see me?*

There was no time to figure it out. Ella saw Rowan's sword lift into the air, as if by magic. Then Jack's backpack levitated off the ground too. But how would they get back across the courtyard without being seen?

"Stop!" someone shouted.

Too late, Ella realized. They had already been spotted.

A teenaged boy stood only a few feet away. He held out his hand as if to keep them from running, but as Jack's backpack zipped open—all by itself—the boy's eyes grew wide. When he turned to alert the other villagers, Ella felt Taiga stiffen by her side. He began to growl.

"No, Taiga," Ella whispered. "Don't hurt him. He's not a mob. He's a boy—a boy like Jack."

But that *boy* was about to blow their cover. And if they didn't get out of there fast, they'd end up back in the jail cell in the basement of the blacksmith's shop.

The boy raised his hand to his mouth, about to call for help.

Then Ella heard a *yowl* and saw a flash of orange fur. The cat pounced, pinning the boy to the ground. She didn't hurt him, but she wasn't about to let him up, either.

When the boy let out a cry of surprise, Ella felt a tug on her arm.

"C'mon!" shouted Rowan. "Run!"

As they raced past the well, Ella felt eyes upon her. And when she glanced down, she realized why. Her legs were visible—only her legs. Wait, now her hands were too. The potion was wearing off!

At her feet, she saw a silver tail and Taiga's paws, racing across the earth. And up ahead, Rowan's red ponytail sailed through the air behind her invisible head.

"Run!" Rowan called again as she glanced over her shoulder, which had suddenly reappeared.

Ella heard footsteps behind her. The villagers were running now, too, giving chase.

Out of the corner of her eye, she saw Jack's hand digging in his backpack. He pulled out a bottle and unstopped the cork.

"Jack, no!" she cried.

What was in the bottle? What kind of damage would it do? "These are villagers, not mobs!" she cried again. *Even if they're chasing us. Even if they're angry!*

But Jack didn't listen. He hurtled the bottle through the air. It hit the ground beside the well, releasing a cloud of bubbles, forming a magical curtain. And one by one, the villagers ran through it.

Lingering potion, Ella realized. Jack had used it in the Taiga, too, to fight the zombie pigmen. To *harm* them.

Was he harming the villagers too?

As they plowed through the curtain of bubbles, the villagers kept running—as if in slow motion. Their arms and legs moved, but ever so slowly. Like Rowan, back in the swamp, when she'd been hit by the witch's potion.

"Potion of slowness!" Ella cried out.

And Jack, whose face was fully visible now, smiled wide.

The potion wouldn't harm the villagers, but it would sure slow them down.

When Ella reached Gran, she and her cousins kept running. Gran wouldn't let them stop. And as Ella looked up, she saw that the flock of parrots was moving with them.

The birds rose from the village like a cloud of dust or a swarm of angry bees. And then they began to fly, following Ella and her family.

Away from the jungle village.

Alongside the stream.

Back toward the swamp.

Toward home, Ella realized. *I'm so ready to go home!*

CHAPTER 15

"In here!" Gran called from the entrance to the cave. "Come inside. Hurry!"

They had made it to the water's edge, and walked for an hour along the steady stream. But the sun was sinking again—already. And mobs would be spawning soon.

Gran lit a torch and began clearing leaves and twigs from the floor of the damp dugout.

As Ella stepped inside, she searched all the shadowy spaces, checking for cobwebs or glowing red eyes. Listening for a *hiss* or a *groan*. She didn't want to be surprised by a mob again, not after everything that had happened on this journey.

Rowan must have felt the same, because she quickly piled stones near the entrance—to keep unwelcome guests out. Then she spread out her cape on the ground like a picnic blanket, and Gran pulled some bread and fish from her backpack.

But when a *mew* sounded from outside, Ella leaped back up. She quickly rolled a stone away from the entrance, gazing through the crack like a peephole. When she saw what was outside, she pushed more stones away, clearing a path.

Jack's ocelot stood in the doorway.

"You can come in," she said soothingly. But the cat wouldn't move—until Jack squatted and held out his hand. Then slowly, cautiously, she stepped into the cave.

This time, Taiga didn't growl or even bark. He didn't so much as whimper.

"Good boy," Ella whispered, giving his neck a scratch.

"Who's this now?" asked Gran, holding her torch high above the spotted ocelot. "Would you like to introduce us, Jack?"

"She's mine," Jack said proudly. "But she's hurt."

He pointed toward the broken arrow. Gran studied it, as if seeing it for the first time. And her face changed. "I think I know this cat," she whispered.

Jack's head swung around. "You do?"

Gran nodded slowly. "I recognize her now. She belonged to your mother."

What? Ella tilted her head. Had she heard Gran right?

"She was hurt during the Uprising," whispered Gran. "She's carried that broken arrow for nearly eight years."

Ella's stomach clutched. Had this cat been with Jack's mother when she died? *Did the ocelot take an arrow trying to protect her person, the way Taiga nearly took an arrow today for me?* she wondered. Her throat tightened, and she reached again for her wolf.

The cat brushed past Gran's legs, as if to say, *Hello again. It's been a long time.* Then it stretched out on the floor next to Jack and began to groom its fur.

Jack looked as if he couldn't quite catch his breath. "What did my mother call the cat?" he asked. "What's her name?"

Gran smiled. "Ask her," she said. "Maybe she'll tell you."

As Jack gazed into the ocelot's green eyes, she gave a slow, contented blink.

"Lucky," he said, sitting back up. "Her name is Lucky."

Gran nodded. "Very good, Jack. She was your mother's good-luck charm. And now, maybe she'll be yours too. She helped us today, didn't she?"

Jack nodded and slowly stroked the cat's head until she purred. "Can we help her too?" he asked, pointing toward the arrow.

Gran stared thoughtfully. "I hope so," she said. "We'll try, when we get home. But remember—you're the healer, you with your powerful potion of Healing. Your mother would be proud, Jack."

He nodded, and unzipped his backpack. "I collected everything I could," he said. "Everything her journal told me to find."

As he dumped the contents of his pack onto the ground, Ella gazed in wonder.

Slimeballs.

A bottle of gunpowder.

Carrots.

Cocoa pods.

Pufferfish.

Sugar cane.

Spider eyes. *Gross!*

A gold ingot.

At the sight of the ingot, Ella remembered the treasure chest. "Jack found me this book too!" she said, digging it out of her pack. "For enchanting Rowan's trident." She held up the book, which lit the cave with its purple glow.

"And my saddle," said Rowan. "Jack found that too." She patted the saddle, which she was leaning against like a chair.

"Did he now?" asked Gran. "Maybe soon, that saddle will get some use." She winked at Rowan.

Would Rowan find her horse, the way Jack had found his ocelot? The way Gran had found her parrots?

Gran's parrots were gone now. They had settled onto a fallen log at the edge of the jungle, bobbing their heads up and down as if saying goodbye.

"The jungle is their home," Gran had said. "But they'll be right here, if we need them again."

Gran summoned an army of birds, thought Ella. *Will my cousins and I lead great armies of animals one day too? Like Gran, and like our parents?*

Ella didn't ask the question out loud. The thought excited her—but also terrified her.

Then she caught sight of Rowan's trident leaning against the cave wall. *I didn't think I could fight with it,* Ella remembered. *But when the skeletons came, I did.*

Her gaze flickered over to Jack, who was sorting his potion ingredients. *I didn't think he could survive out here all on his own, with nothing but his potions,* she remembered. *But he did!*

So maybe, just maybe, they would both lead great armies one day. And what about Rowan?

Ella looked at her red-headed cousin and grinned. *Yes. Rowan too. Especially brave Rowan.*

But for now, Ella was content to curl up with Taiga, in a warm cave lit by Gran's torch, with the family she loved most—all of them, together now.

She buried her face in her wolf's warm fur and sighed.